PUFFIN BOOKS

UPSIDE DOWN STORIES

Annabelle the cow saves a ship from disaster while
Bert the tiger spends all day in the bath; and the Moon
gets an overcoat, and an apple tree grows squirrels.

Here is a surprising and funny collection of Donald
Bisset's nonsense tales, taken from *Time and Again
Stories*. Everything is upside down and the wrong
way round – and guaranteed to keep you amused.

Donald Bisset is a professional actor and writer, and is
well known for his brilliant nonsense tales. His *Talks
with a Tiger* is also published in Young Puffin.

D1343537

Also by Donald Bisset

TALKS WITH A TIGER

Donald Bisset

·

UPSIDE DOWN STORIES

Illustrated by Alison Claire Darke

PUFFIN BOOKS

PUFFIN BOOKS

Published by the Penguin Group
27 Wrights Lane, London W8 5TZ, England
Viking Penguin Inc., 40 West 23rd Street, New York, New York 10010, USA
Penguin Books Australia Ltd, Ringwood, Victoria, Australia
Penguin Books Canada Ltd, 2801 John Street, Markham, Ontario, Canada L3R 1B4
Penguin Books (NZ) Ltd, 182–190 Wairau Road, Auckland 10, New Zealand

Penguin Books Ltd, Registered Offices: Harmondsworth, Middlesex, England

First published by Methuen in *Some Time Stories*, 1957,
and *This Time Stories*, 1961
This selection published in Puffin Books 1987
Reprinted 1988

Copyright © Donald Bisset, 1957, 1961, 1987
Illustrations copyright © Alison Claire Darke, 1987
All rights reserved

Filmset in Trump Mediaeval (Linotron 202) by
Rowland Phototypesetting Ltd, Bury St Edmunds, Suffolk

Printed and bound in Great Britain by
Cox & Wyman Ltd, Reading

Except in the United States of America,
this book is sold subject to the condition
that it shall not, by way of trade or otherwise,
be lent, re-sold, hired out, or otherwise circulated
without the publisher's prior consent in any form of
binding or cover other than that in which it is
published and without a similar condition
including this condition being imposed
on the subsequent purchaser

Contents

•

1. The river of words

Once upon a time there was a river which was made of words. It flowed down to the sea and the sea was made of story books.

As the river flowed along, the words and the letters tumbled over each other and buffeted the rocks just like ordinary rivers.

'I know,' said the river. 'Let's write a story! Once upon a time . . .'

'Hurray!' shouted all the other words. 'That's the way to begin a story. Now what comes next?'

This is the story the river told them.

Once upon a time there was a river made of words and it was going down to the sea and all the words were going into story books, when suddenly a little otter swam across the river and the words got into the wrong order so that instead of writing 'Once upon a time' it wrote 'on a Once up time' and it got in a frightful muddle.

'Oh, you are a naughty otter,' the river said to the otter whose name was Charlie. 'Now you've spoilt our story.'

'I'm terribly sorry!' said Charlie. 'Perhaps if I swim back again it'll put things right.'

He swam back and then clambered on the

bank and looked at the words, 'time upon a Once', he read. 'Surely that's not right!'

However the river swirled about a bit and soon got it right. 'Once upon a time,' he read, 'there was an otter whose name was Charlie.'

'Why that's me! My name's Charlie. It's a story about me!' He got so excited and jumped up and down and then slipped and fell in the river and jumbled up the words again. Oh, the river was annoyed!

The otter got out as quickly as he could and looked at the words: 'otter was Charlie time upon a Once'. Worse and worse!

'What do you expect?' said the river. 'Every

time we start you fall in and get it all jumbled. Now we've got to start all over again.'

'Once upon a time there was an otter whose name was Charlie and he lived by the river of words . . . Now what happens next?'

They thought and thought but couldn't think of a story about Charlie. So he said, 'I'll help,' and got back from the river and then ran as fast as he could and jumped right into the middle of the river. Then he swam ashore and looked at the words. (He'd jumbled them right, this time.)

'Once upon a time there was a very naughty otter,' he read, 'and one day he met a pussy-cat.'

'Miaow!' said the pussy-cat. 'Do you like ice-cream?'

'No!' said Charlie.

'Miaow! Do you like milk?'

'No!'

'Miaow! Do you like fish?'

'Yes, I do!' said Charlie.

'Miaow,' said the pussy-cat. 'Well, if you come to my house my auntie will give you a fish tea. Brown bread and butter and fish paste.'

'That will be nice!' said Charlie. 'It makes me feel quite hungry. I think I'll go home to tea now. But before I go tell me, what are you going to do with the story?'

'It's going to be a story in a book called *Time and Again Stories*,' said the river.

Charlie was pleased. 'That's nice!' he said. 'Now I'm going! Goodbye!'

'Goodbye!' said the river.

The words all jumbled around and then spelt 'Love and kisses to Charlie'. And tumbling and tossing they flowed on into the story-book sea.

2. The thin king and the fat cook

Once upon a time there was a very fat King who said to his very thin cook, 'Bake me a cake! The lightest, nicest, scrumpiest cake you've ever made.'

So the cook got a big bowl and two dozen eggs and some butter and five pounds of flour and a pound of yeast.

He mixed the flour and the eggs and the butter in the big bowl, then put in the yeast. Then he lit the gas and when the oven was hot he put the cake in.

Soon there was a lovely smell of baking cake, and the King came running in.

'My, my!' he said. 'What a lovely smell. I'm sure it's going to be a delicious cake, cook.'

'Ah yes, Your Majesty,' said the cook. 'And it's going to be the lightest cake in the world, I put in a whole pound of yeast to make it rise.'

'That's the stuff!' said the King. 'But what's this?' They looked round and saw that the top of the gas stove was beginning to bend and suddenly, with a *Crack!* it shot up in the air and the top of the cake appeared, rising slowly.

'Tch, tch!' said the King. 'Now, look what you've done! You put in *too much* yeast!'

The cake went on rising until, at last, it was pressing against the ceiling, which began to crack.

The cook and the King rushed upstairs and when they got to the top they saw the cake had gone right through the ceiling to the floor above.

'Do something, my good man!' shouted the King. The poor cook didn't know what to do. So he jumped up and sat on the cake to stop it rising.

But it went on rising just the same till the cook felt his head bump on the ceiling. A moment later his head went through the roof and still the cake went on rising.

'Oh, Your Majesty! Please go and turn the gas off!' shouted the cook.

The King rushed downstairs and turned the gas off. Then he got his telescope and went into the garden.

The cake had stopped rising, but the top was very high up in the air.

'Oh, drat the man!' said the King. 'If he doesn't come down soon there won't be anyone to cook the dinner.' Then he thought, 'If the cook was to start eating the cake, then he would get lower and lower.' So he called out, 'Cook, eat the cake, at once!'

'Delighted, Your Majesty,' called back the cook, and he took a bite. 'Yum, yum!' he said. 'This *is* nice cake!'

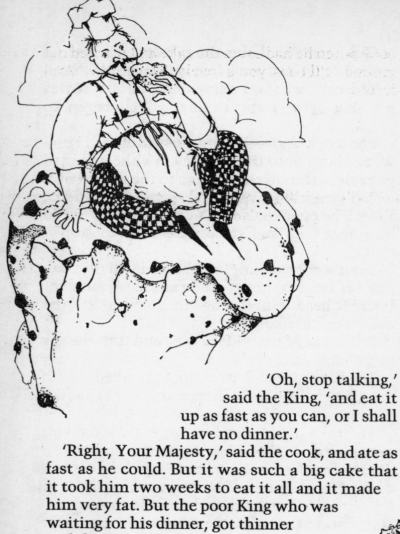

'Oh, stop talking,'
said the King, 'and eat it
up as fast as you can, or I shall
have no dinner.'

'Right, Your Majesty,' said the cook, and ate as
fast as he could. But it was such a big cake that
it took him two weeks to eat it all and it made
him very fat. But the poor King who was
waiting for his dinner, got thinner
and thinner.

So instead of the King being fat
and the cook being thin, there was
a very thin King and a very fat cook!

'Never mind, Your Majesty,' called the

cook when he had eaten the cake and reached the ground. 'I'll cook you a lovely dinner now!' And he did.

3. *St Pancras and King's Cross*

Once upon a time there were two railway stations who lived right next door to each other. One was called St Pancras and the other King's Cross. They were always quarrelling as to which was the better station.

'I have diesel engines as well as steam engines at my station,' said St Pancras.

'Humph! So have I!' said King's Cross.

'And I've got a cafeteria,' said St Pancras.

'So have I!'

'Open on Sundays?'

'Yes, open on Sundays!'

'Humph!'

There was silence for a few minutes, then King's Cross said, 'Well, I've got ten platforms and you've only got seven.'

'I'm twice as tall as you are!' replied St Pancras. 'And, anyway, your clock is slow.'

The King's Cross clock was furious and ticked away as fast as it could to catch up. It ticked so fast that soon the St Pancras clock was away behind, and it ticked as fast as it could too, so as not to be outdone. They both got faster and faster; and the trains had to go faster too so as not to be late.

Quicker and quicker went the clocks and faster and faster went the trains, till at last they had no time even to set down their passengers, but started back again as soon as they had entered the station. The passengers were furious and waved their umbrellas out of the windows.

'Hi, stop!' they called. But the engines wouldn't.

'No!' they said. 'We can't stop or we'll be late. Can't you see the time?'

By now the clocks were going so fast that almost as soon as it was morning it was evening again.

The sun was very surprised. 'I must be going too slow!' it thought. So it hurried up and set almost as soon as it had risen and then rose again. The people all over London were in such a state getting up and going to bed, and then getting up again with hardly any sleep at all – and running to work so as not to be late, and the children running to school and hardly having time to say twice two are four and running home again.

Finally the Lord Mayor of London said to the Queen, 'Your Majesty, this won't do! I think we ought to go and give a medal to Euston Station, then the other two will be so jealous they may stop quarrelling.'

'That's a good idea!' said the Queen. So she set out from Buckingham Palace with the Lord Mayor and the Horse Guards and the Massed Bands of the Brigade of Guards, and in front of her walked the Prime Minister carrying a gold medal on a red velvet cushion. When they got to King's Cross the two stations stopped quarrelling and looked at them.

'Do you see what I see, St Pancras?' asked King's Cross.

'I do indeed!' said St Pancras. 'A medal being taken to Euston Station, just because it's got fifteen platforms. It's not fair! Why, you're a better station than Euston!'

'And so are you, St Pancras,' said King's Cross.

St Pancras was surprised, but it thought it would be nice to be friends after all the quarrelling, so it said, 'Let's be friends.'

'Yes, let's!' said King's Cross.

So they became friends and stopped quarrelling, and their clocks stopped going too fast and their trains stopped having to hurry. Everyone was very pleased.

'You are clever, Lord Mayor!' said the Queen.

'Thank you, Your Majesty,' said the Lord Mayor.

4. The winding road

Once upon a time a little blue car was going along a winding road.

'Why are you so bendy?' it said to the road.

'Well,' said the road, 'shall I tell you the story of how I was made?'

'Yes, please!' said the little blue car. 'Tell me the story.'

'Well,' said the road, 'some men with pickaxes and shovels made me. I started off straight, and, after a little while, I met a cow who was lying asleep so I said, "Wake up, Cow! I'm the new road just being made. I want to go straight and you are in the way."

'The cow opened her eyes and said, "Moo!" But she wouldn't go away, even though the men went and shouted in her ear. So they built the road (that's me) round her; and that was the first bend.

'Then, when they had gone a little farther, a bull in the field bellowed at the men very fiercely so they turned away, and that was the second bend.

'After that one of the men said, "I would like a nice ice-cream!"

'"So would I!" said the others.

'So they bent me round to the place where the ice-cream shop was and they each bought an ice-cream, and that was the third bend. Then they all lay down to sleep.

'When they woke up the foreman said, "Now, lads! Let's be getting on with it!" So they got up and started again, but they were still so sleepy they didn't notice where they were going and went the wrong way around another bend. That was the fourth!

'"Hi!" said the big foreman. "You're going the wrong way. We're supposed to go that way!" And he pointed a different way. So they turned a fifth bend and went that way.

'After a while they saw a hen who had a family of chickens.

'"Will you please move your chicks?" said the men. "They are in the way."

'"Well, there's one more egg to hatch yet," said the hen.

'"Oh no!" said the men. "That will take too long!" So they built me round them.

'By then it was nearly time to go home, so they put their pickaxes and shovels away and the foreman looked at me. "You're not very straight, are you?" he said. "Oh well, never mind!" And then he went home.

'So you see, little blue car, that's why I am so bendy,' said the road.

'I do see!' said the little blue car. 'I do like bendy roads. Toot-toot!'

5. The tiger who liked baths

Once upon a time there was a tiger whose name was Bert. He had big, white, sharp teeth and when he growled it made a noise like thunder.

But Bert was a very nice tiger, always kind and gentle, except when someone else wanted to have a bath.

He loved having a bath and lay in the water all day until Mr and Mrs Smith and their baby daughter, who lived

with him, were very cross. Because every time they wanted to have a bath Bert growled and showed his teeth.

'Come on, Bert! Do come out and have your supper,' said Mrs Smith, holding out a big plate of bones.

'No, thank you,' said Bert, and growled.

Poor Mrs Smith nearly cried. 'It's time to bath the baby,' she said, 'and there's Bert still in the bath. Whatever shall I do?'

'I know what we'll do,' said Mr Smith, and he went and bought twenty bottles of black ink and, when Bert wasn't looking, he poured them into his bath. It made the water all black so that Bert got all black too.

A few hours later Bert decided it was supper-time so he got out of the bath.

'Oh, look at that big black pussy-cat,' said Mr Smith.

'Oh yes, what a beautiful pussy-cat!' said Mrs Smith.

'Pussy-cat?' said Bert. 'I'm not a pussy-cat. I'm a tiger.'

'Tigers have stripes,' said Mr Smith. 'They are not black all over like you.'

'Oh dear!' said Bert. 'Perhaps I am a pussy-cat after all.'

'And pussy-cats,' said Mr Smith, 'don't like having baths. You know that!'

'That's true!' said Bert.

After supper Bert went into the garden. And Prince, the dog next door, who liked chasing pussy-cats, saw Bert, and said, 'There's a pussy-cat! I'll chase him!'

He felt a bit nervous because Bert looked the biggest pussy-cat he had ever seen. Still, pussy-cats had always run away before when he barked at them so he ran up to Bert, barking and showing his teeth.

Bert turned his head lazily and growled just once, like this: GRRRRRRRRRRRR!

Prince had never been so frightened in his life, and he jumped over the fence and ran home.

A little later, when Mr Smith came into the garden, Bert asked him, 'Am I really a pussy-cat? Don't you think I'm too big?'

'Well, you're not *really* a pussy-cat,' said Mr Smith. 'You're a tiger. A special kind of tiger, who never likes staying in the bath for more than half an hour. And that's the very best kind of tiger.'

Bert *was pleased*. 'That kind!' he said to himself. 'The very best kind!' And he purred and then licked all the black off till he was a lovely yellow tiger again with black stripes.

Then he went into the house and said to Mr Smith, 'I think I'll just go and have a bath.' And he turned the water on and had a lovely bath. But he stayed in the water only for half an hour, and Mrs Smith said he was a very good tiger and gave him a big bucket of ice-cream.

Bert put his head in the bucket and licked. 'Yum! yum! yum!' he said. 'I do like ice-cream.'

6. Annabelle

Once upon a time there was a cow with a poorly tummy. Her name was Annabelle. And one day she saved a big ship from being wrecked.

One foggy day, on the coast of Cornwall, Annabelle was in her field eating some grass for breakfast. The fog was so thick that she couldn't see the end of her nose, and suddenly she swallowed a thistle.

Oh dear! It was in her tummy and prickled and hurt like anything. Annabelle stopped eating and mooed as loudly as she could.

Just then a big ship was sailing by on her way to America.

The Captain looked through his telescope but he could see only fog.

'Do you know where we are?' he said to his first officer.

'No, Sir! But we're somewhere off the coast of Cornwall.'

'Well, sound the hooter,' said the Captain. So the first officer sounded the hooter – 'Moooo!'

Annabelle heard it, and thought, 'There's another cow who has swallowed a thistle. I must

get the doctor,' and she mooed to let the other cow know she had heard.

'Listen!' said the Captain. The first officer stopped sounding the hooter and listened. Then, from across the water, through the fog, they heard it again: 'Moo!'

'That's Annabelle Cow,' said the Captain. 'We must be near her field.' And he started giving lots of orders.

'Stip the shop! I mean – stop the ship!'

'Reverse the engines!'

'Drop the anchor!'

'Sound the hooter!'

The ship stopped, the anchor chain rattled down, the ship's siren sounded again: 'Moooo!'

'Oh, what a poorly tummy that cow's got,'

thought Annabelle, and she mooed again, 'Moooo!'

The Captain looked over the side. Soon the sun came out and the Captain saw that he had stopped the ship from hitting a big rock.

He had saved his ship, all because he had heard Annabelle's moos.

Just then, he heard her mooing again, 'Mooooo! Mooooo!'

'That's funny,' he thought, 'she's still mooing, perhaps she's got a poorly tummy!' So he sent the ship's doctor ashore to make Annabelle's tummy better.

'And give her this too!' he said, and handed the doctor a little box with a big label tied to it.

When the doctor reached the shore, Annabelle was still feeling poorly, but he gave her some pills and she soon began to feel all right.

'The Captain asked me to give you this,' said the doctor. He took the little box the Captain had given him and showed it to her. On the label was written:

'To Annabelle – The Cow that saved our Ship – From the Captain.'

Inside was a lovely silver medal. The doctor tied it round Annabelle's neck and the medal hung on her chest. She *was* proud.

'That's because by mooing you saved the ship. Now I must hurry back because we are going to America,' said the doctor.

He hurried to the ship. The sun shone brightly and the fog had gone.

Annabelle looked out to sea.
'Moo!' she said.
'Moo!' replied the ship.

As the ship sailed on, the moos became fainter.
But the Captain, looking through his telescope,
could see Annabelle eating grass with the medal
round her neck.

'Moo!' said Annabelle, looking out to sea.
'Moo!'

And from the big ship, far across the water, she
thought she heard a faint 'Moo!'

She was very happy and went on eating her
grass, while the medal shone in the morning
sunlight.

7. The horse and the apple tree

Once upon a time there was a little apple tree that was just growing up. One day a horse came along and decided that he'd wait there till some apples had grown and then have a good meal.

'I'll eat your apples for you!' said the horse to the tree. The tree felt glad at first, then it began to be worried.

'I'm not quite sure how to grow apples!' it thought. So it asked a thistle that was growing near by, and the thistle told the tree how it thought apples should be grown.

The tree took the thistle's advice and, in the autumn, it grew not apples – but thistles.

It was very upset. And so was the thistle, who had meant well. The horse was even more upset. 'I'll have to wait till next year, now, for apples!' he thought.

Well, the next year the tree was determined to grow apples properly and one day, when a squirrel was scampering along its branches, it asked the squirrel how *he* thought apples should be grown. The squirrel told it and it took the squirrel's advice and, that year, it grew not apples –

but squirrels, who wriggled till they dropped on to the ground and scampered away.

The tree and the horse were both upset. So one day, when the farmer, whose tree it was, came along with his wife, the tree swished its leaves in the wind. The farmer pointed to it and said, 'This little apple tree grew thistles in its first year, squirrels in the second year. I wonder what it will grow this year?'

'Fancy, a squirrel tree!' said his wife. 'Perhaps it doesn't know how to grow apples.'

'Hm! That's true!' said the farmer, and went on to say how *he* thought apples should be grown. And his wife agreed with him.

The tree listened very carefully and took their advice, and next year, grew not apples – but babies.

The farmer's wife was pleased. She was very fond of babies. 'They're so nice to cuddle!' she said. 'And they smell all milky.'

But, presently, they began to cry. What a noise they made!

After that the horse became very thoughtful. 'I wonder,' he said out loud, glancing at the tree, 'I wonder what's the best way to grow horses?'

The tree thought for a bit, then it told the horse how *it* would grow horses. The horse listened very carefully and remembered everything the apple tree said. And one day, soon after, when the tree asked, 'Dear horse, please tell me, how would *you* grow apples?' the horse looked at the

tree and told it word for word exactly what *it* had said about how to grow horses.

'I'll take your advice!' said the tree and for the first time, felt rather more sure of itself.

'Aha! you're taking your own advice!' thought the horse. 'And that's how it should be!'

The horse was quite right, for the very next autumn, the tree bore loads of lovely red apples.

'Ah!' said the horse. 'I do like apples!'

8. The puddle and the bun

Once upon a time there was a little puddle on the pavement. It had been raining and the water was still dripping from the glistened leaves on the trees. People walked by and a passing bus was reflected red in the water.

'Well, this is life,' thought the puddle. 'It's better than living in a cloud. All the same, I wish someone would drink me. After all, that's what water's for!'

Just then a great big van full of currant buns came along and, as it passed, one fell off with a splash right into the puddle.

'Dear, oh dear me,' said the bun. 'Now I'm all wet and no one will eat me. I do feel sad!' And it began to cry.

'Oh, please don't cry,' said the puddle. 'Please don't cry.'

'You're very kind,' said the bun. 'But, you see, though it's nice here with all the people passing and the red buses, and the trees dripping water, it's not so nice for a bun as being eaten, and I was on my way to the cafeteria at the station. I was going to be sold as a station bun and eaten with a cup of tea. Oh dear. Oh dear.'

'Now don't cry,' said the puddle. 'Don't cry, dear bun!'

'I won't!' replied the bun. 'I'm glad to have met you. Wouldn't it be fun if someone would come along and eat me and drink you?'

'Oh yes,' said the puddle. 'But look . . . Can you see what I see?'

There, coming towards them, was a mother duck and three little ducklings. A policeman put up his hand to stop the cars and buses while they crossed the road.

'And where are you going?' asked the policeman.

'Quack!' said the mother duck. 'We're going to the pond.' And all the little baby ducks said, 'Squeek squeek squeek!' and followed their mother across the road.

'Oh, I do feel tired!' thought the mother duck. 'And all the children should have a rest and something to eat.' Then she saw the currant bun and the puddle. 'Quack quack quack!' she said. 'Look, there's a lovely currant bun and a puddle!' They were pleased!

'Goodbye, dear puddle,' said the bun.

'Goodbye, my dear,' replied the water.

'Yum yum yum,' said the little ducks. 'We do like buns and puddle water.'

The buses passed, people walked by, and as the sun went down, the rain dripped from the trees and made a new puddle on the pavement, and the stars, coming out one by one in the sky overhead were reflected in the water.

'Honk honk honk,' said the buses.

'Quack quack quack,' said the baby ducks.

'Drip – drip – drip,' went the rain.

And that is the end of the story.

9. The Emperor's mouse

Once upon a time, long, long ago, there lived an Emperor. This Emperor had a little mouse whose name was Misha.

Misha lived in the Emperor's pocket, and sometimes he came out and ran about the room and up the Emperor's sleeve.

One day, when the Emperor was sitting on his throne telling people what to do, a messenger arrived and bowed very low and said, 'Your Majesty! Your mother is coming to tea and she is bringing her cat, Suki, with her.'

'Oh dear!' said the Emperor. 'Suki is the best mouser in the whole of the empire. She'll be sure to catch Misha. Whatever shall we do?'

Just then some trumpeters outside blew their trumpets.

'It's your mother,' said the messenger. 'She is here already!'

'Quick!' said the Emperor. 'Pass me that thick envelope.'

He got some scissors and cut some holes in it. Then he took a pen and addressed the envelope to himself. At the bottom in big letters he wrote: WITH CARE – DO NOT DROP.

Then, just as his mother and Suki were coming up the path, the Emperor stuck a stamp on the envelope. He put a little bit of cheese inside it. Then he took Misha out of his pocket and put him in the envelope and stuck it down.

'Now hurry out the back way,' he said to the messenger, 'and post this.'

Then the Emperor kissed his mother and said, 'Would you like some tea?'

'Yes, please!' she said. So he gave her some.

Meanwhile Suki was prowling around sniffing everywhere, to see if she could find a mouse to catch. But she couldn't.

Next day, after his mother and Suki had gone home, the postman came to the palace with a letter for the Emperor.

'It's a very wriggly letter, Your Majesty!' said the postman.

The Emperor took it and smiled. 'I *wonder* what's in it?' he said. He opened it — and there was Misha inside, quite safe.

40

'I *am* glad to see you, Misha,' said the Emperor, holding the mouse in his hand. And then he put him in his pocket.

10. Bath night

Once upon a time there lived a beautiful black beetle whose name was Joe. He lived with his mother and father and fourteen sisters and eleven brothers in a crack in the wall of a big house.

He was the eldest beetle, and used to help his mother on bath nights by washing and scrubbing and drying and polishing his brothers and sisters.

Then, when they were all tucked up in bed, he used to go for a walk in the garden and smell the flowers and have a talk with the other beetles or caterpillars or any friendly creature.

But one day, as he was walking across the grass, it started to pour with rain and Joe got very wet. So he thought, 'I'll just go and sit in front of the fire in the sitting-room in the big house and get dry before I go home.'

He crawled in, and there in front of the fire, he saw all the letters of the alphabet drying themselves. It had been their bath night too.

There was big A with a towel, drying all the little letters who had come down from the bathroom where big G had given them a bath. When they saw Joe they all crowded round him.

'What's your name?' they asked.

'Joe,' said Joe.

'Shall we spell it for you?'

'Yes, please!' said Joe who had never yet tried to spell his name.

'Come on,' called big Y. 'Who's first?'

Big J jumped up on to the hearth; then little o; and then little e. And all the letters clapped. After that they had a lovely game of spelling. It was their favourite game. (The only one they knew, really!)

'Come on,' called big K, 'let's spell "dog".' So little d and little o and little g got up and stood in a row and all the letters clapped again and d, o and g bowed.

'Now, let's spell "cat",' said big K. And c—a—t stood in a row.

'Now spell "cake",' said big G. So little c and little a stood up again and so did little e. But, where was little k? He wasn't there! Some of the letters looked under the carpet. Big Y ran upstairs and looked in the bathroom. They searched everywhere, but they couldn't find him. Then Joe had an idea and he went out into the back yard. He looked at the place where the waste water-pipe came down from the bathroom and there he saw little k stuck in the grating.

Joe pulled him out and brushed him and took him back to the fireside. The letters *were* pleased. Then Joe said he had to go home because it was bedtime and big K said, 'Would you like some cake crumbs?'

'Yes, please!' said Joe. So they gave him a bag of crumbs.

'Do come and see us again,' said the letters, 'any evening after the children have gone to bed.'

'I will,' said Joe, and he carried the cake crumbs home and gave one each to his mother and father and brothers and sisters. Then he kissed them all good-night and crawled to his own little part of the crack in the wall and went to sleep.

11. How the star-fish was born

Once upon a time there were seven elephants.

There was a great big elephant and a not-so-big elephant, and an elephant who wasn't quite as large as that, and a middle-sized elephant, and one a bit smaller, and a very small elephant and a tiny little baby elephant.

They were all standing on top of a hill near the seaside watching the stars shine. The night was very dark and the stars twinkled brightly.

The fish in the sea were watching the stars too. And whenever they saw a falling star, they dived under the water to look for it because it seemed to them to have fallen into the sea.

'Let's try and catch a falling star,' said the great big elephant.

'Oh yes, let's!' said the others.

So the great big elephant picked up the not-so-big elephant in his trunk, and the not-so-big elephant picked up the elephant who wasn't quite so large as that, and the elephant who wasn't quite as large as that picked up the middle-sized elephant, and the middle-sized elephant picked up the one who was a bit smaller, and the elephant who was a bit smaller picked up the very small elephant, and the very small elephant picked up the tiny little baby elephant.

Then the great big elephant threw all the others out into the sky towards a falling star. And when they had gone some way the not-so-big elephant threw the others farther still. And when they had gone some way the elephant who wasn't quite so large as that threw the middle-sized elephant and the other three as far as *he* could. And then the middle-sized elephant threw the one who was a bit smaller and the other two. And then the one who was a bit smaller threw the very small elephant and the baby elephant. And when they had nearly reached the falling star, the very small elephant threw the tiny little baby elephant; and the tiny little baby elephant caught the falling star in its trunk and gave it to the very small elephant, and the very small

elephant gave it to the one who was a little larger, and the one who was a little larger gave it to the middle-sized elephant, and the middle-sized elephant gave it to the next biggest elephant, who gave it to the next one, and he gave it to the great big elephant, who gave it to a fish who swallowed it and it became a star-fish.

12. Please, Thank-you
and Sorry

Once upon a time, Please and Thank-you were having a little talk. They were feeling very sorry for themselves. Presently they saw Sorry coming along.

'Why is it,' said Sorry, 'that all the other words have such a nice easy time while we have to work so hard? People are always saying, "Please", "Sorry" and "Thank you", but half the time they don't mean what they say. It isn't fair!'

'No, it *isn't* fair!' said Thank-you. 'There is a lady in our street who has a little girl and she is always saying, "Say thank you" to her. I'm sure that when that little girl grows up she will say "thank you", but it won't *mean* much. And it makes me so very tired. I just don't get a moment's sleep.'

'It's just as bad for me,' said Please. 'All day long, in every bus in the world, it's "Fares, please! Fares, please! Fares, please!" Of course, it's nice being polite, but I am quite worn out.'

Please turned to sit down and accidentally trod on Thank-you's toes. 'Sorry!' he said.

'There you go!' said Sorry. 'Even you make me work!'

'Oh, sorry!' said Please. 'I trod on Thank-you's toes so I said sorry, Sorry.'

'There you go again!' said Sorry. 'Will you please stop it? There, now I'm making *you* work. What shall we do to get a rest?'

They thought for a bit and then decided they would go for a nice long holiday and sleep for a whole week. Then no one in all the world would be able to say 'Please' or 'Sorry' or 'Thank you'. And that's what they did.

When they came back from their holiday, they weren't feeling tired any more, and they didn't mind when all the people started to say 'Please' and 'Sorry' and 'Thank you' again. It seemed *much* nicer because people had got out of the habit of mumbling 'Please' or 'Sorry' or 'Thank you' whether they meant it or not. They only used the words when they really and truly wanted to say them, so Please, Sorry and Thank-you did not have to work quite so hard, and were not nearly so tired as they used to be.

Every year now, they go away for a holiday so that when they come back, people will remember when they say 'Please' or 'Sorry' or 'Thank you' that the words really do mean something.

13. The Captain's horse

Once upon a time there was a horse who had very short legs. His name was Dick.

He was a very nice horse, but sometimes the other horses laughed at him; and once, when he was trotting along, a little worm who was crawling by, said, 'Hahaha! Look at old shorty legs!'

And a little black duck swimming on the pond quacked, 'Poor thing, he *has* got short legs, hasn't he!'

Dick felt very sad, 'I wish I had nice long legs,' he thought. 'What use is a horse with short legs? Boohoohoo!' And he began to cry.

Presently he saw a soldier sitting under a tree by the roadside and he was crying too. Tears were streaming down his cheeks and making his black moustache all wet.

'Oh dear, what's the matter?' said Dick, going up to him.

'The King says I can't have any jam for tea!' said the soldier, sobbing louder than ever.

'No jam for tea!' said Dick, feeling very sorry for him. He saw that the soldier was wearing spurs on his boots and was carrying a helmet that had a big dent in it.

'No!' sobbed the soldier, whose name was Henry. 'The King said that next time I dented my helmet I wouldn't have any jam for tea. Every time I ride under the archway out of the castle, I bang my head on the roof and dent my helmet. But I can't help it! My horse has got such long legs that I'm too high up. I wish I had a horse with nice short legs like – like you!' he said, looking at Dick's short legs. 'Will you be my horse?'

'Of course I will!' said Dick. And they gave each other a big hug. Henry took Dick to the castle and gave him some hay.

Next day the King ordered his buglers to blow their trumpets. So they blew, 'Tarrarara tarrarara!' and all the King's soldiers got on their horses, rode out of the castle and lined up in a row, waiting for the King to come out.

When he came out he saw that everyone except Henry had a dent in his helmet and he was very angry. But first he asked Henry, 'How is it you haven't got a dent in your helmet?'

'Because, Your Majesty,' said Henry, 'I've got a horse with nice short legs – his name's Dick.'

'Why, so you have!' said the King. 'Yes! Very nice short legs.' Then he called out to the other soldiers, 'You're very naughty to dent your helmets. You shan't have any jam for tea today. And in future, you must all ride horses with nice short legs like Dick here.'

Then he told Henry he was made Captain of the Guard. And he gave Dick a new nosebag with his name on it. He was a very happy horse.

14. Hide-and-seek

Once upon a time the Dark was playing hide-and-seek with the Moon. Sometimes it hid behind houses or chimneys and kept very still while the moonlight crept round to find it.

Sometimes it would dart about, hiding behind a pussy-cat or a little dog crossing the road. It was very clever at hiding from the Moon.

But when the Sun rose, that was different.

'Just you wait!' said the Moon. 'When the Sun shines where will you hide then?'

'I'll hide behind the children going to school,' said the Dark, 'and be their shadows.'

'That's all very well,' said the Moon, 'but when the children go *into* school, *then* where will you hide? Really, my dear, you had better go and hide round the other side of the world or the Sun will be sure to catch you.'

'No, it won't!' said the Dark. 'You wait and see!'

Well presently the Sun rose and most of the Dark went and hid round at the other side of the world and made it night there, but some little bits of Dark stayed to play with the Sun.

They had a lovely time and some pieces were

people's shadows and some were pussy-cats' shadows and dogs' shadows and cows' shadows, and some were little birds' shadows and flitted across the lawn, but the Sun nearly always caught them in the end till there was only one little piece of Dark left.

'I'll catch you!' said the Sun. 'No matter where you hide!'

'No you won't!' said the Dark. 'I've thought of a lovely place where you'll never find me. Now don't look! And count ten while I go and hide.'

So the Sun hid behind a cloud and counted ten. Then it came out to look.

'I expect it's hiding behind someone and being their shadow!' said the Sun. But though it looked everywhere, it couldn't find the Dark.

It looked all day and all the next day, but couldn't find it, and indeed it never found it at all because the Dark had found such a wonderful place to hide – in the cupboard under the stairs.

'It is nice here!' thought the Dark. 'I think I'll stay here all the time.' And it did.

And that's why it's always dark in the cupboard under the stairs.

15. The squeak

Once upon a time in the Festival Hall in London, a lady was dancing and all the people in the audience were watching and having a wonderful time. But the dancer herself was rather angry because, every time she stepped on one floorboard on the stage, it squeaked.

So after the dancing was over, she said to the manager, 'There is a floorboard on this stage that squeaks every time I tread on it. How can I dance when the floorboard squeaks?'

'Oh, I'm terribly sorry!' said the manager. 'I'll mend it.' And after the people had gone home, and it was all dark in the theatre, the manager collected lots of nails and went out on the stage with a lighted candle. He put the candle down, and hammered the board absolutely *all* the way round so that it couldn't *possibly* squeak any more.

Next day, when the dancer came, the manager said, 'Madam, my dear, I have nailed the floorboard down so that it cannot squeak any more.'

'Thank you!' said the dancer. 'You *are* a nice manager.'

Well, the people came in and the music played

and she started to dance again, but every time she stepped on that board – it *squeaked*.

As soon as the curtain came down for the interval, she sent for the manager and she said, 'I thought you said you had stopped that board squeaking! Well, listen!' And she trod on the board – and it squeaked. She trod again – and it squeaked again.

'Now,' she said, 'just take that board away and get one that doesn't squeak.'

So the carpenter came along and the manager came with some nails and hammers and saws, and they cut the board and they picked it up and were just going to throw it away when they saw in the space underneath it, a little teddy bear.

'Oh, what a lovely teddy bear!' said the dancer, and she picked it up and gave it a hug. And as soon as she gave it a hug – it *squeaked*.

'Oh!' she said. 'Now I understand! Whenever I trod on the board it made *you* squeak.'

Everybody laughed. And they put the board back and the music played and the dancer danced beautifully and made all the people happy.

That night, the dancer took the teddy bear home. When she got there her little boy was sound asleep and she put the teddy into his cot.

In the morning he woke up and saw it. 'Look!' he said. 'There's a teddy bear in my bed!' And he gave it a hug – and it squeaked.

16. Starry eagle

Once upon a time an eagle, whose name was David, lived on top of a mountain in Wales.

David liked flying high up in the air. One day he flew so high that he came to a star. There was a little house on the star. Mary and her little lamb lived there. David knocked on the door.

'I've come to tea,' he said. So Mary laid the table and they all sat down.

'Would you like some toast, Eagle dear?' said Mary.

'Mm – no thank you,' said David, 'I'd like to eat a little lamb.'

'My! you haven't washed your claws,' said Mary, and she picked David up and took him through to the kitchen to wash. While he was drying his claws she came back and whispered in the little lamb's ear.

David came back and sat down.

'Would you like some more toast, little lamb?' said Mary.

'No, thank you,' said the lamb, remembering what Mary had whispered to him. 'I think I'd like some eagle.'

David was surprised, and felt a bit nervous. So

when Mary asked him again what he would like, he said, 'I think I'd like some toast, please.' So Mary gave him some. And after tea he said good-bye to Mary and her little lamb, and flew all the way home again.

Before he went to sleep that night, he looked up and saw the star shining high above him.

17. Snow

Once upon a time, long, long, ago, there lived a little girl who had never seen the snow. Her name was Lin, and she lived in China.

One day, when Lin was walking in the garden with her pussy-cat whose name was Cheng Pu, she felt sad.

'I feel sad, Cheng Pu,' she said.

'Miaow!' said Cheng Pu, as if he understood.

'You know, I've never seen the snow, and I *would* so like to.'

'Miaow!' said Cheng Pu again.

That evening, in the garden after Lin had gone to bed and no one was near, the flowers began to talk to each other.

'Fancy,' said a tall yellow hollyhock to a little blue pansy, 'Lin has never seen the snow. She is so kind and waters us every day. I wish we could help her.'

'I know what to do,' said the South Wind, who was blowing there. It blew far, far away to the North across deserts and mountains and green valleys until, at last, it came to the North Pole where the North Wind lived.

'What are you doing here?' shouted the North Wind when it saw the South Wind. 'Go away, or I'll chase you!'

'Ha, ha, ha!' laughed the South Wind. 'You can't catch me!'

'Oh, can't I,' roared the North Wind. 'We'll soon see about that.' And it chased after the South Wind.

But the South Wind turned round and blew all the way back to China, and the North Wind followed as fast as it could. But it couldn't catch the South Wind. It *was* cold though, and the clouds all shivered when the North Wind came by, and they stopped raining – and snowed.

When the North Wind found it couldn't catch the South Wind, it went back to the North Pole in a horrid temper, and blew so hard that even the polar bears shivered.

Next morning when Lin came into the garden, she saw it was covered with snow.

'How softly white and beautiful everything is!'
she said. 'Come and look, Cheng Pu. It must be
snow!'

'Miaow!' said Cheng Pu.

Soon the South Wind blew and melted the
snow, and the sun came out and warmed the
flowers. Lin was very happy.

18. The policeman's horse

Once upon a time there was a very naughty police horse whose name was Harry, and a rather naughty policeman, too, whose name was Arthur.

Arthur, dressed in his blue uniform with his truncheon by his side, used to ride through London mounted on Harry the horse.

Harry liked following the buses that crawled slowly along in the traffic and breathing on the back window till it was all misty. Then Arthur

leant forward in the saddle and, with his finger, he would draw faces on the misty window, which made Harry laugh.

But they were so busy, Harry following the buses and breathing on the window, and Arthur drawing faces, that they never had time to catch any burglars. So the inspector at the police station, whose name was Reginald, said to the police sergeant one morning, 'Sergeant!'

'Yes, sir!' said the sergeant, standing to attention and saluting.

'Sergeant,' said Reginald, 'why doesn't Arthur catch any burglars?'

'I don't know, sir,' said the sergeant.

'Well, find out, Sergeant, there's a good chap,' said Inspector Reginald.

'Yes, sir!' said George (that was the sergeant's name), and saluted again. Then he went out and got on his horse, which was a very good horse and never breathed on the back of buses, and rode down the street to see if he could find Harry and Arthur and see what they were up to.

Then he saw them. There was Harry breathing on the back window of a bus to make it misty and Arthur leaning forward and drawing a picture on it.

'Oh, they *are* naughty!' said Sergeant George. 'Still, it would be rather fun, wouldn't it?' So he edged his horse up behind a bus so that it breathed on the back window. Then he leant forward and drew a picture of Inspector Reginald on the glass with his finger. And another policeman saw him and thought it would be fun, too. After that, all the policemen's horses started to follow buses and breathe on the windows so that the policemen riding them could draw pictures.

And all the burglars were very surprised because the policemen were so busy drawing that they never came to arrest them any more.

'I wonder what has happened to the policemen?' they said, and they went and looked and saw that they were drawing on the windows on the backs of the buses.

'What fun!' said the burglars, and they all went and stopped being burglars and bought horses instead so that they could breathe on the bus windows for them to draw pictures too.

The head policeman of all London was very

pleased about that, so he sent for Harry and Arthur.

'You are both very clever!' he said, and made Arthur a sergeant.

19. The Moon's overcoat

Once upon a time, on a cold winter's night, the Moon was looking down at the world. Everyone was wearing a warm overcoat.

'I would like one, too,' it thought. So it said to the Man-in-the-Moon, 'Will you make me a warm overcoat, please?'

'All right!' said the Man-in-the-Moon. So he got out his sewing machine and some cloth and some thread and some buttons and his scissors and tape measure.

First of all he measured the Moon, then he cut the cloth and sewed it up. Then he put on the buttons. Within a fortnight the coat was ready, and he said, 'Now, come and try it on.'

The Moon tried it on, but it was much too big.

'That's funny!' said the Man-in-the-Moon, scratching his head. He got out his tape measure and measured the Moon again. It was much smaller this time. So he got his scissors and sewing machine and thread and made the coat smaller.

A fortnight later, when he'd done the alteration, the Moon tried it on once more. This time it was much too small because somehow the Moon had grown fatter.

'How can I make you an overcoat that fits if you keep getting fat and thin like that?' said the Man-in-the-Moon. He was quite angry, but being a kind man he said, 'I'll make you two overcoats. One for when you are fat and one for when you are thin.'

'Thank you!' said the Moon.

When the coats were made it tried them on and

they fitted very well. But of course, when it had an overcoat on, it couldn't shine properly.

When the people in the world looked up they could see the stars shining, but they couldn't see the Moon, and they felt sad.

'That will never do!' said the Man-in-the-Moon. 'You must shine sometimes so that the children going to bed can see you.'

'All right!' said the Moon and took off its overcoat and shone.

The people down in the world looked up and saw it and were very pleased, especially the children. Sometimes they saw the Moon was fat and sometimes it was a thin crescent moon, and sometimes they couldn't see it at all.

'Ah!' they said. 'It's got its overcoat on.'

'Yes,' said the Moon. 'I have! And it's lovely and warm.'

But it didn't keep it on for long and soon shone again, high up in the sky away above the clouds. When the little stars heard about the Moon's overcoat they were very interested.

'Let's go and ask the Man-in-the-Moon to make us overcoats,' they said.

'Oh no!' said the Man-in-the-Moon. 'I couldn't possibly make an overcoat for every star in the sky. It would take me years and years and *years*. Besides, I haven't enough material.'

Then he had an idea and he called to all the little clouds. He told the clouds to go and wrap themselves round the stars at night and keep them warm.

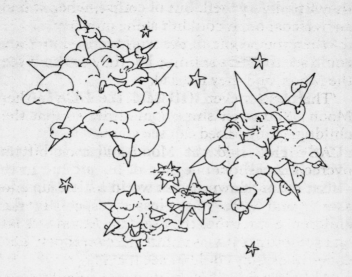

The stars were thrilled. But when the Moon took off its overcoat and started shining by itself, it grew lonely. So whenever the Moon took off its overcoat, the stars would give the clouds a night off. And then they winked and twinkled their hardest at the Moon. The Moon was very pleased. And so were all the people down in the world below, especially the children.

20. The thoughtful beetle

Uncle Fred lived at No. 8 Westwind Road, Whitechapel. On one side of his picture in the front room there stood a rose in a little glass jar,

and on the other, a clock whose name was Tyma.

'What a useless thing a clock is,' said the rose to itself, 'it doesn't smell at all. Only things that smell nice are really beautiful.'

'What a foolish thing a rose is,' thought the clock, 'it doesn't show the time, and only things that tell the time are really beautiful.'

Just then a black beetle walked by, and he looked at the rose and the clock.

'Hmmm! they are not very black, are they?' he thought. 'Poor things!' and he walked on. He was going to see his grandmother – it was her birthday.

Then a sparrow looked in at the window and saw the clock and the rose. 'Huh! what's the good of ticking and smelling if you can't fly? What is more beautiful than flying?'

'Swimming,' said a goldfish, who was in a bowl of water at the other side of the room.

'Miaowing,' said a cat, jumping from the windowsill into the garden.

'Eating,' said a pig who lived in a sty in the garden next door.

'Making the trees wave,' said the wind, as it rushed down the garden path.

'Making the wind blow,' said the trees, as they waved at the bottom of the garden.

The rose and the clock were still arguing when Uncle Fred came in with his wife.

'And what are you good for?' they said to him.

'Well,' said Uncle Fred, 'it all depends on how you look at it I suppose.'

'Of course it does,' said his wife. 'I think you are nice to kiss,' and she kissed him.

Some other Young Puffins

THE GHOST AT NO. 13
Gyles Brandreth

Hamlet's sister Susan is perfect in every way – she is the cleverest, the most perfect, in fact the goodiest goodie-goodie Hamlet has ever met. He tries very hard to like her but it is difficult to like someone so special when you're so ordinary. Then something extraordinary happens to Hamlet that Susan just won't believe – and Hamlet spends the summer holidays making a very spooky friend.

ZOZU THE ROBOT
Diana Carter

Rufus and Sarah found the Thing in the garden. It looked like a ball, but it buzzed, it changed colour, and it *talked* – or at least the thing inside it did. Zozu turns out to be a tiny metal creature, not a bit like the huge scary visitors from space that they had always imagined. They grow very fond of their little friend – and what exciting adventures they have together!

RADIO DETECTIVE
John Escott

Laura still tunes in to Roundbay Radio even though her dad has banned it from their house. She even enters their poetry competition, first making sure that no one will ever know. But she hasn't counted on the determination of Donald, the programme's young presenter, who sets out to discover the mystery prize-winner and finds out more than anyone expected.

ON THE NIGHT WATCH
Hannah Cole

At the end of term the classrooms and playground will be locked and never used again. But no one is happy with the idea of sending all the children to different schools, and so teachers, parents and pupils get together to draw attention to their cause, all determined to keep their school open. Can the council be persuaded to change its mind? There is a very effective way of forcing them to listen . . .

THE THREE AND MANY WISHES OF JASON REID
Hazel Hutchins

Eleven-year-old Jason is a very good thinker. So when Quicksilver (no more than eighteen inches high) grants him three wishes, he's extremely wary. After all, in fairy tales, this kind of thing always leads to disaster. So Jason is absolutely determined to get *his* wishes right. But it's not that easy, and he lands himself and his friends in all sorts of terrible but funny scrapes!

MR BERRY'S ICE-CREAM PARLOUR
Jennifer Zabel

It is thrilling enough to have a lodger in the house – after all, not even Andrew Brimblecombe has a lodger – but Carl is over the moon when he discovers that Mr Berry plans to open an ice-cream parlour.

DINNER AT ALBERTA'S

Russell Hoban

Arthur the crocodile has very bad table manners, until he is invited to dinner at Alberta's.

MARGARET AND TAYLOR

Kevin Henkes

Seven simple stories featuring Margaret and Taylor, a brother and sister whose competitive relationship leads to lots of amusing and instantly familiar domestic incidents.

THE ELEPHANT PARTY AND OTHER STORIES

Paul Biegel

A circus elephant gives a wonderful party, a witch's shoe punishes a cheeky boy, and lots more in these eleven enchanting stories, both funny and fantastical.